A Special Something

For Antonia Rose

And to the memory of Joyce—
a brave and beautiful lady

For information address Hyperion Books for Children,
114 Fifth Avenue, New York, New York 10011-5690.

Printed at Oriental Press, Dubai, U.A.E.
First published in Great Britain by Metheun Children's Books,
an imprint of Egmont Children's Books Limited.

First U.S. Edition 2000
1 3 5 7 9 10 8 6 4 2

Library of Congress Cataloging-in-Publication Data
Fearnley, Jan. A special something / Jan Fearnley.
p. cm.
Summary: A little girl imagines what strange things
could be inside her mother's tummy.
ISBN 0-7868-0589-7
[1. Pregnancy—Fiction. 2. Babies—Fiction. 3. Imagination—Fiction.] I. Title.
PZ7.F2965Sp 2000
[E]—dc21 99-36646

Visit www.hyperionchildrensbooks.com, a part of the GO Network

A Special Something

Jan Fearnley

HYPERION BOOKS FOR CHILDREN
NEW YORK

My mommy is wonderful. She has a big fat tummy,
and she waddles around, tired and slow.

"What do you have in there?" I ask.

"A Special Something," Mommy tells me, patting her bump. "Come closer and see."

I look at her tummy. It's huge! There must surely be a hippopotamus in there!

Oh, no! A big fat hippopotamus will take up all the room in the wading pool. . . .

and hog all of my toys!

"Oh, Mommy, it's not a hippopotamus, is it?"
"No, silly. Put your ear to my tummy and listen."
Woofity-boom . . . woofity-boom . . . woofity-boom goes
the Special Something.

Oh, no! It's a big dinosaur with a drum! He'll bang, bang, bang with it all night long and keep me awake and I'll be late for school, and my teacher will be so mad at me.

"Mommy, is it a dinosaur with a drum,
by any chance?"

"No, dear. Come and give me a nice cuddle." So I climb up next to Mommy and give her a cuddle.

Wriggledy-jiggle! Wriggledy-jiggle! Wriggledy-jiggle! goes the Special Something.

Aaah! There's a big, wriggly crocodile in there!
He'll wriggle and jiggle the table . . .

and ruin all of my drawings! And then I'll get in
trouble for making a mess!

"Is it a crocodile, Mommy?"

"No, my pet. Come and put your hand here. Quick, you can feel something moving."

Well, there's something moving, all right! *Kick, kick, kickety-kick!* goes the Special Something.

Things are getting worse! It's an angry
kangaroo that'll steal my ball to play soccer.

And he's bound to kick the ball so hard it'll land
in the neighbor's yard and spiteful Gillian will take it
away into her bedroom. And it's my only one!

"Mommy, is it an angry kangaroo?"

"No, love. But it is time for your story now."

I choose my story, and snuggle up with Mommy and Daddy. But halfway through, when I'm just about to decide if I'm sleepy, the Special Something joins in, too. *Nudge-nudge! Nudge-nudge! Nudge-nudge!*

Well! It must be a monkey. A hairy, naughty monkey, with big pointy elbows! It'll nudge me in class and I'll get into trouble for fidgeting.

It'll tease me when I'm trying to eat my breakfast nicely,

or when I'm doing my best to be good in the back of the car.

I go off to bed, very worried indeed. . . .

When I wake up, there's Gran, stroking my hair.
"Mommy's gone to fetch your Special Something,"
she says. And off we go to see her.

Mommy sits up high in her hospital bed.
She cradles something in her arms.
"Look what we have here," Daddy says.
I climb up on the high bed and peek
inside the yellow blanket.

Is it a hippopotamus?

A dinosaur?

Or a crocodile?

Is it a kangaroo?

Or a monkey?

It's my baby brother. "It's our Special Something, Mommy!"
Mommy hugs me close, and now I can hold him, just like her.
He doesn't go *woofity-boom*, or *wriggledy-jiggle*, or *kickety-kick*, or even
nudge-nudge. And he doesn't look much like a hippopotamus.

My little brother sleeps cradled in my arms, safe and soft and new, and makes hardly a sound. Then he opens his eyes and looks at me.

Daddy smiles at us both and takes a picture. . . .

"Of my two Special Somethings."